Brooke and Binky

NO MORE BINKY!

by Jill Treyes

Brooke and Binky: No More Binky
ISBN: 0-88144-339-5
Copyright © 2009 by Jill Treyes

Published by
Yorkshire Publishing Group
9731 East 54th Street
Tulsa, OK 74146
www.yorkshirepublishing.com

A little girl named Brooke loved her binky,
especially while reading a book.

**All morning, noon, and night, her binky never left her sight.
During breakfast, lunch, and dinner, Brooke's binky was always with her.**

Naptime, bath time, playtime....even during bedtime!
Brooke would say her binky was "Mine, mine, mine!!!"

Mommy and Daddy thought very long and hard to find a way for Brooke and binky to part. Brooke loved her binky and would not let go, but it was time for Brooke to just say no.

"No more binky!" as Mommy would say.
But Brooke cried and cried until she had her way.

**Months and months later, Brooke and binky remained together.
As Brooke grew bigger and bigger, she still needed her binky with her.**

So Mommy and Daddy hugged her close and tight,
"It's time to let go Brooke, it'll be alright!"

Brooke was brave and left her binky behind.

But she kept looking for it, and binky was no where to find.

As Brooke started pre-school, she learned to play, laugh, and run.
Without her binky all day, Brooke still had lots of fun.

Brooke came home that day with a great big smile, looking for her binky because it had been awhile. "Wow!!" Mommy said, "Your smile is very pretty. Let's show off that smile with no more binky!"

**Brooke loved her binky but learned to let go.
With no more binky, her smile can now show.**

Both Mommy and Daddy were very proud, how Brooke learned to let go without a pout. Mommy and Daddy hugged her so very tight, knowing Brooke's a big girl now, she'll be alright!!

**No more binky!! No more binky!!
Brooke gave it up and swore on her pinky!**

Brooke showed her pretty smile, day after day.
As she no longer needed binky, she went on to play.

**She smiled so big, and would sing to herself, "Laaah....lah..lah...lah...lah...."
She played with her friends.....Ella, Niko, Mel, Brandon, and Kayla.**

CPSIA information can be obtained
at www.ICGtesting.com
Printed in the USA
LVIC06n1055280217
525663LV00007B/12